The GINGERBREAD DOLL

by Susan Tews • Illustrated by Megan Lloyd

Clarion Books • New York

Clarion Books
a Houghton Mifflin Company imprint
215 Park Avenue South, New York, NY 10003
Text copyright © 1993 by Susan Tews
Illustrations copyright © 1993 by Megan Lloyd

Printed in the U.S.A.

Library of Congress Cataloging-in-Publication Data
Tews, Susan.
The gingerbread doll / by Susan Tews ; illustrated by Megan Lloyd.
p. cm.
Summary: Although her family's prosperity brings her increasingly
nice dolls as Christmas gifts, Rebecca is most fond of her
gingerbread doll because it was made from love.
ISBN 0-395-56438-7
[1. Dolls—Fiction. 2. Christmas—Fiction.] I. Lloyd, Megan,
ill. II. Title.
PZ7.T29647Gi   1990
[E]—dc20   90-2642   CIP   AC

WOZ 10 9 8 7 6 5

My grandmas and aunts
get together each winter
for a day of baking Christmas cookies.
When the oven's hot and full
and the kitchen smells spicy
my great-grandma Rebecca tells us her story
of the gingerbread doll.
It happened in 1930
during the Great Depression
when people were terribly poor.
She was only nine years old,
living on a farm in Wisconsin.

She remembers boots crunching
through the snow surrounding the narrow farmhouse.
Her mama had to feed the animals,
even on Christmas morning.
Rebecca pulled the blankets around her
to fight off the chill.
She was the first one awake except for her parents.
Heat from the stove barely reached the upstairs bedrooms.
That's why Mama had tacked cardboard over the window.
Rebecca pulled it out a little to see.
Frost patterns iced the glass,
and it would have been a perfect Christmas picture
except for the way her mother struggled
with the heavy bucket.

Mama had been so full of hope
that last winter when they'd bought the farm.
She and Daddy had saved a long time.
They packed all their belongings
into a borrowed truck
and the two boys rode with Daddy.

The other five children went in the car with Mama.
Rebecca kept the baby warm under her coat
while they drove from Illinois through a snowstorm.
It took them all night and part of the next day
to get to the rocky fields of their new home.

Rebecca remembered when her mother
first saw it was a tarpaper house.
Mama almost cried.
The house looked like some patched-up black stovepipe.
The plumbing was frozen,
and inside, the floor and walls were a mess.
Daddy set his jaw and painted WILCOX on the mailbox.
It was only some miracle
that got them through the winter.

Hail destroyed most of the first year's crop.
Daddy said it would be a lean Christmas.
But the holiday excitement kept Rebecca hoping
she'd find a porcelain doll under the tree,
the doll she'd seen in the store window in town.

Her little sister Claire woke up.
"What're you lookin' at?"
"Just Mama," Rebecca said.
Claire jumped out of bed. She said,
"Come downstairs to see our presents!"
There wasn't much under the tree.
Rebecca let go of her hopes for a doll
when she saw that all the packages were small.
They were wrapped in brown paper and string.

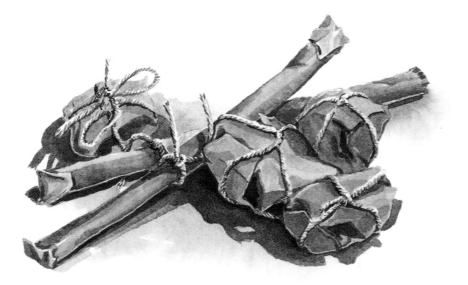

Her oldest brother James read off the names.
Rebecca and the older children
made a fuss over each gift
so the little ones wouldn't notice
they were just things like walnuts and pencils.
Daddy held on to Mama's hand.

Rebecca felt a lump in her throat.
There was no gift for her.
Then Mama looked at her face
and went to get something from the cupboard.
"I couldn't get you that doll you picked out,"
she said, "not this year anyway,
but I did have a little molasses and lard.
It got me to thinking,
and I baked you a gingerbread doll."

A gingerbread doll?
Who had ever heard of such a thing?
But Rebecca's heart leaped when she saw it.
She was good at imagining
and she knew it would serve just fine—
more than just fine—as a doll.
Mama had rolled the dough extra thick
and used a knife to cut out the shape of a girl.
She'd stuck in pieces of yarn for hair.
Then she'd stitched together
scraps of cloth for a dress.
Finally Mama had sewed on three different shiny buttons.

Rebecca knew right away what to name her.
"Button Marie," she announced. "That's her name."
She cradled Button Marie like a baby doll.
Mama had made her just for Rebecca.
And Rebecca took extra care not to break her
because a gingerbread doll
is every bit as delicate as porcelain.

For breakfast they had a treat,
gingerbread pieces soaked in cream.
Mama laughed when Rebecca said,
"Nobody better be thinking about
eating my Button Marie for breakfast!"

Rebecca would take the doll's dress off
and put it back on gently
and twirl her yarn hair into a curl.
She kept her in a box lid
on top of the girls' chest of drawers.
She liked to prop her up against the wall.
Rebecca still would have given anything
to have that porcelain doll,
but she loved Button Marie in a way
you could never love anything from a store.

One day Rebecca opened the drawer too fast,
and before she could catch her
Button Marie hit the dresser top hard.
Rebecca wanted her mother to glue her.
Mama studied the broken pieces in her lap
and managed a smile.
"Honey," she said, "Button Marie wasn't meant
to last forever. She was just a cookie."

Rebecca cried. "She was not just a cookie!
You said she was a doll!"
"She was a doll because you loved her,"
her mother said, touching Rebecca's hand.
Sadly Rebecca put away Button Marie's dress.

The next year there was a good harvest
and the family filled the loft with hay.

James and Daddy nailed beautiful white siding on the farmhouse.
That Christmas the presents had colored wrappings.
Times were getting better.

Rebecca felt sure she would never love another doll
as much as she had Button Marie,
but her gift that year was a cornhusk doll.
The neighbor ladies taught Mama
how to soak the husks and bend them just so.
Mama used a fine-tipped ink pen to draw a face,
and she made the doll so beautiful
that Rebecca did love her.
She gave Mama a great big kiss.

After another year
Rebecca got a store-bought cloth doll.
It wasn't as nice as a porcelain one,
but she liked the cloth doll's pink ruffled gown.
For fun she would put Button Marie's dress on her.
When Mama saw the gingerbread doll's dress
she said, "Where did you get that old thing?"
but her eyes sparkled when she said it.

Mama taught the children to pinch pennies
so they'd know how to get by when times were hard.
Daddy never got rich, but he did well enough farming.
At last, one Christmas
Mama gave Rebecca a porcelain doll.
She was a beautiful doll with ruby lips,
dressed in red satin and white lace,
with ringlets of chestnut-colored hair.

But Rebecca also kept Button Marie.
Now she's just a scrap of cloth and buttons
that my great-grandma smooths out with her thumbs.

She shows her to me on cookie-baking day,
and Great-Grandma Rebecca tells me
she was her best doll.

She says, "Button Marie was made from love,
and that's the part of a gingerbread doll
that lasts forever."